The Fabled Stables

WILLA THE WISP

BY

JONATHAN AUXIER

ILLUSTRATED BY

OLGA DEMIDOVA

AMULET BOOKS · NEW YORK

The Library of Congress has cataloged the hardcover edition as follows:
Names: Auxier, Jonathan, author. | Demidova, Olga, illustrator.
Title: Willa the wisp / by Jonathan Auxier ; illustrated by Olga Demidova.
Description: New York : Amulet Books, 2020. | Series: The Fabled Stables ; book 1 | Audience: Ages 6 to 9. | Summary: One day eight-year-old Auggie Pound, the caretaker of the rare animals in the Fabled Stables, ventures into the swamp to save a new rare creature, the wisp.
Identifiers: LCCN 2020025368 | ISBN 9781419742699 (hardcover) | ISBN 9781419742712 (paperback) | ISBN 9781683357834 (ebook)
Subjects: CYAC: Imaginary creatures—Fiction. | Animals, Mythical—Fiction. | Friendship—Fiction.
Classification: LCC PZ7.A9314 Wi 2020 | DDC [Fic]—dc23

Paperback ISBN 978-1-4197-4271-2

Text copyright © 2020 Jonathan Auxier
Illustrations copyright © 2020 Olga Demidova
Book design by Steph Stilwell and Heather Kelly

Published in paperback in 2022 by Amulet Books, an imprint of ABRAMS.
Originally published in hardcover by Amulet Books in 2020.

Printed and bound in China
10 9 8 7 6 5

Amulet Books are available at special discounts when purchased in quantity for premiums and promotions as well as fundraising or educational use. Special editions can also be created to specification. For details, contact specialsales@abramsbooks.com or the address below.

Amulet Books® is a registered trademark of Harry N. Abrams, Inc.

ABRAMS The Art of Books
195 Broadway, New York, NY 10007
abramsbooks.com

FOR PENELOPE,

MATILDA, AND HAZEL

Girt with a boyish garb for boyish task,

Eager she wields her spade: yet loves as well

Rest on a friendly knee, intent to ask

The tale he loves to tell.

—Lewis Carroll

AT THE TOP OF THE WORLD SAT AN ISLAND.

And at the heart of that island lived a boy
named Auggie.

Everyone is good at something. Auggie was good at
caring for animals. Wherever he went, turtles peeked
from their shells, birds hopped closer, and worms
wriggled up from the ground.

In most ways, Auggie was just like other children, except for one thing: Auggie had a *job*.

Most jobs are boring, grown-up things, but not Auggie's job.

Auggie worked at the Fabled Stables!

The Fabled Stables looked very small from the outside, but on the inside . . .

The stables were filled with one-of-a-kind
creatures. Some were magical. Some were mysterious.
Some were just plain *weird*.

Auggie marched between the stalls. He sang,
"Come big! Come small! Come breakfast for all!"
The hungry herd rushed to meet him.

Animals can be picky eaters.
Luckily, Auggie had a magical
Horn of Plenty. All he had to do
was reach inside and pull out
the exact food that each beast
loved best.

5

He fed the Hippopotomouse . . .

The Bush Squid . . .

The Long-Beaked Curmudgeon . . .

6

The Yawning Abyss . . .

Auggie loved his amazing beasts, and they loved him right back. (That didn't stop a few of them from trying to eat him.) But just like each of these creatures, Auggie was one-of-a-kind.

He was the only boy on the island.

And even the best job in the world can get lonely without a friend.

"Do you think the Whompus ever feels lonely?" Auggie said.

"So what if she's lonely?" muttered Fen. "At least she's not facedown in a pile of dung."

Fen was also one-of-a-kind. He was a thing called a Stick-in-the-Mud. He could make himself into any shape Auggie needed to do his job. Right now, Auggie was using Fen as a rake.

"Maybe you and I could be friends?" Auggie said.

Fen rolled his eyes. "I'll take my chances with the dung."

2

AFTER BREAKFAST CAME HURLY-BURLY HOUR. Auggie opened the stable doors. "By branch or stream or field or track, I'll see you all for mid-morn snack!"

Beasts galloped and slithered and flapped and skittered all over the island. Animals in the Fabled Stables were never locked up. They were free to roam wherever they pleased. There were no cages or leashes or collars.

While the beasts hurly-burlied, Auggie went to visit Miss Bundt in the Plotting Shed. Maybe she would play with him?

"Ahoy, Auggie!" Miss Bundt called with a hearty smile. She had the sort of smile that made you want to smile back.

Auggie sat next to her. "Can you tell me the story of one of your tattoos?" He was pretty sure that Miss Bundt used to be a pirate. But she would never admit it.

"I'm afraid I can't right now." She cinched a knot with her teeth. "I'm working on this ladder for Professor Cake. He needs it finished by moon-up."

The whole island belonged to a man named Professor Cake. He was very old and very clever. He collected things that were one-of-a-kind. Things like Auggie.

Auggie looked at the ladder. He couldn't see the end. "Why does the Professor need such a big ladder?"

"Your guess is better than mine!" Miss Bundt
wiped her brow. "I learned not to bother asking the
Professor 'why' a long time ago."

Auggie nodded and sighed. "Sometimes I wish
Professor Cake was a bit *less* mysterious."

"Aye, you and me both."

Auggie watched Miss Bundt work. He wondered if
she felt lonely, too. He was about to ask her if she had
any friends before she came to the island, when—

BOOM!

The stables SHOOK and
SHUDDERED and TWITCHED
and SPUTTERED.

3

A MOMENT LATER, EVERYTHING WAS SILENT. Auggie watched as the doors of the stables gently swung open, as if they were inviting him inside.

"What just happened?" Auggie said.

Miss Bundt helped him up. A look of worry snitched across her brow. "Seems like you should find out."

Auggie stepped into the waiting stables. They felt different than before. The air smelled musky. The ground felt soft. The wooden beams were creaking gently, as if the walls themselves were breathing.

At the end of the row was a new stall that Auggie didn't recognize. "That stall wasn't here this morning. I'm sure of it."

Fen hopped to his side. "Of course it wasn't here this morning. Don't you know *anything*? We have a new arrival."

New arrivals were nothing new. Sometimes Auggie would wake up to discover that the stables had rearranged themselves. There would be a new stall and a new beast to care for. But this felt different. This felt urgent.

"I've never seen the stables change in the daytime like that," Auggie said. "It must mean something."

Fen sniffed. "It means there will be even more dung to shovel."

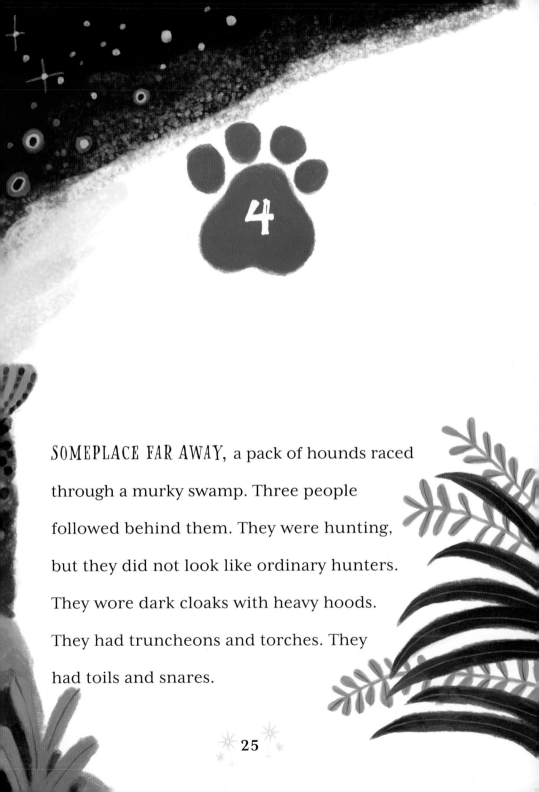

4

SOMEPLACE FAR AWAY, a pack of hounds raced through a murky swamp. Three people followed behind them. They were hunting, but they did not look like ordinary hunters. They wore dark cloaks with heavy hoods. They had truncheons and torches. They had toils and snares.

The tallest hunter peered through a spyglass.

"Spread out! It can't have gone far."

A pale blue light flicker-flashed between the trees.

"There it is!" another hunter shouted. "After it!"

The hounds
SNARLED and
SNAPPED and

SPLASHED
after their prey!

5

BACK ON THE ISLAND, Auggie approached the new stall. The inside looked different from the rest of the stables. Instead of wooden walls, he saw a moonlit swamp. It stretched out as far as he could fathom. It was like a window to another world—

someplace far, far away.

There was a sign over the gate:

"What's a wisp?" Auggie asked.

"Only one way to find out." Fen propped an elbow on the gate. "Someone has to go in there and get it."

Auggie clutched Fen's twiggy hand. "We . . . we have to go *into* that dark swamp?" He did not like the dark very much.

"*We*? You're on your own, kid!" Fen pulled free of his grasp. "The last time I left the island, a giant tried using me as a toothpick. I still have nightmares." He shuddered. "My job is cleaning, and your job is caring. That means *you've got to go in there and do it yourself.*"

A hungry HOWLLLLLLL rang out from the darkness.

"Sounds like you'd better act quick," Fen said. "The stables wouldn't have made this stall unless this wisp was in serious trouble."

Auggie peered into the swamp. He wasn't sure he was ready to leave the safe, warm stables. What if he got lost and couldn't find his way back?

I need some way to retrace my steps," he said. But what could he use?

Auggie looked around the stables.

He got an idea . . . a brilliant, bread-crumby idea.

He crept over to the Gargantula, who was sleeping in her web.

"Are you crazy?" Fen whispered. "Never wake a sleeping Gargantula."

"I'm just borrowing some of her thread," Auggie said. He *very carefully* took one end of the Gargantula's web and tied it around his waist.

"Keep an eye on this thread," he said to Fen. "If I pull on it, that means I need you to come help."

Fen folded his branches. "Um, no. If you pull on that thread, it means you're a goner."

Auggie worried that Fen might be right. But then he imagined the wisp all alone in a dark swamp—that creature was depending on him.

He put his pack over his shoulder and took a deep breath. "Away I go."

And away he went.

6

THE NEXT THING AUGGIE KNEW, he was in the middle
of a swamp. Black mud *squished* under his boots. It
was hard to tell where the ground ended and where
the water began.

He could see lights moving through the trees.

"Over there!" A voice shouted. "Don't let it get away!"

Auggie dove out of the way just as . . .

"Catch-as-catch-can!" the thing shouted as it dashed around. It left a faint trail of smoke in its wake.

A pack of hounds broke through the brush, SNARLING and SNAPPING at its tail.

"Ooh!" The thing giggled. "That tickles!"

Auggie opened his pack and looked for something to distract the hounds.

He reached into his Horn of Plenty and pulled out—

A BONE!

The most delicious, mouthwatering, chewable bone that ever was.

The hounds stopped their hunt and stared at the bone in Auggie's hand.

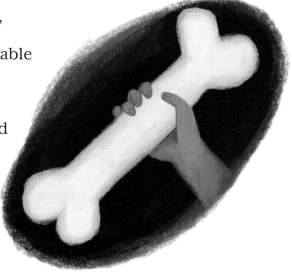

Auggie threw the bone as far as he could. "Fetch!"

With hungry barks, the hounds raced off in search

of the treat.

GRRRRRRR!

"That should keep them busy!" Auggie said.

But when he turned around . . . the creature

was gone!

Auggie looked to the left. He looked to the right.

The creature was nowhere to be found.

Where could it be hiding?

"You can come out now," Auggie said in his

gentlest voice. "I won't hurt you."

There was a flicker in the fog. Auggie saw two long

ears and a pair of big, blinking eyes. "Peekaboo!" she

cried and twiddle-twirled in a circle.

Auggie stared at the creature before him. Her body kept changing in the moonlight—like she was made of mist.

He said, "Are you a wisp?"

"My name is Willa!" Her voice was like breeze moving through branches. "Are you here to play tag, too?"

Auggie thought of those snarling hounds. "Are you *sure* those hounds were playing tag?"

"I think so." Willa scratched behind her ear. "I was only just born tonight. I floated around the trees for a little bit. Then I heard shouting. Then some people and their puppies started chasing me! But they can't catch me! I'm *tricky*!"

"Those people sound like hunters," Auggie said. Hunters were the opposite of caretakers. Even in the thick fog, a glowing wisp would be easy to track. He lowered his voice. "What if I told you I could take you to a secret place where *no one* could find you?"

Willa's face literally lit up. "You mean like hide-and-go-seek?"

"Sort of like that," Auggie said. He took hold of the silver Gargantula thread that led to the stables. They had to get back before those hunters showed up. "Follow me."

A gruff voice shouted "NOW!"

Auggie looked up as a giant net flew through the fog and landed right on top of them!

7

THREE FIGURES STEPPED THROUGH THE TREES.

They wore long robes with strange symbols on them.

The tallest hunter raised his torch. "It seems our

wisp has a friend."

"Finally!" Willa said. "You were taking *forever*!"

"Hands off the wisp," the second hunter said. "It belongs to us."

Auggie shouted, "She doesn't *belong* to anyone!"

The three hunters towered over him. "This is the first wisp we've seen in ages. And we're not going to share it." The third hunter took a strange metal collar from her bag. It had a bell on the end.

Willa drifted through the net. "Ooh! Pretty!"

The hunter clamped the collar around her neck.

Willa laughed. "You think a silly leash can hold me?"

But when she tried to slip through the collar, nothing happened. She pawed and pulled at the metal, but it held fast.

"It burns," she whimpered.

"What did you do to her?" Auggie said.

"The collar is *fraught iron*," the first hunter said. "It counteracts magical creatures. So long as that collar is around the wisp's neck, it can't shimmer free."

Willa's eyes went wide. "You mean I'll be stuck wearing this *forever*?"

Now it was the man's turn to laugh. "Forever?" he said. "You'll be lucky to make it to sunrise."

THE MOON HAD RISEN OVER THE FABLED STABLES.

Fen sat on a bale of hay. He was picking flakes of bark off his elbow.

"Friend!" he muttered. "Who does that boy think he is? I'm a *talking stick*. I don't need friends." Fen had been in the Fabled Stables for a long time. Long enough to know that caretakers came and went.

It was no use getting attached.

Fen eyed the shining strand of Gargantula thread trailing into the wisp's stall. Had it twitched? Just a little bit?

"And I *certainly* don't need to risk my neck in some mucky swamp." It was unclear who he was talking to. It might have been the Gargantula.

Fen stared into the wisp's stall. Before, he

had been able to hear shouts and howling dogs.

But now everything had gone silent.

He wondered if that was a bad sign.

9

AUGGIE WAS STILL IN THE SWAMP. He was cold and tired and scared. He wished he was back in the stables. He wished he was with Fen.

"But I don't *have* any treasure!" Willa told the hunters for the hundredth time. "I was only just born tonight!" Her voice was faint from exhaustion.

"Don't play dumb with us!" One of the men held

up an old book with question marks on the cover.

"Everyone knows wisps lead the way to treasure—now

fess up!"

"She doesn't KNOW." Auggie struggled to get free from his net. "You're just wasting your time."

"Oh, but it's not *my* time." The man pointed overhead. "Take a look at the sky. The moon is nearly gone. Do you know what happens to wisps when the sun comes up? They disappear in a puff of smoke." He pointed at Willa's collar. "If you tell us where the treasure is, I'll set you free. Then you can follow the moon before it's too late."

Auggie didn't know if this was true or a lie. But he knew they couldn't wait to find out. He needed help—fast!

He craned his neck, trying to see if he might find something to help him break free.

But what could he use?

He looked around the swamp. And then he got an *idea* . . . a humongous, hairy idea!

10

AUGGIE TOOK A DEEP BREATH. He called in his loudest voice, "Don't tell them, Willa! No matter what they say, don't tell them about the Thread of Riches."

"The *what*?" said the hunters.

"The *what*?" said Willa.

"Do your worst!" Auggie called. "She'll never reveal the silver *Thread of Riches* that will lead you to her treasure!"

By now all three hunters were standing around him.

The first hunter folded his arms. "Check the book."

Another hunter riffled through the pages.

"Nothing in the book about silver threads."

"Hey, look!" The third hunter picked up the

Gargantula thread. "It's a silver thread."

Auggie made his face look scared. "I'm begging

you! Whatever you do, don't *pull on that thread!*"

The three hunters grabbed hold of the thread and HEAVED.

Auggie heard an angry roar in the darkness.

"That didn't sound like treasure," said one hunter.

"Maybe we should pull harder?" said another.

"Maybe we should—?"

That's when a very grumpy Gargantula BURST

through the trees. "I warned you!" Fen screamed.

"Never wake a sleeping Gargantula!"

CRASHHHH!!!!!

The hunters' eyes went wide as cherry pies. "We should have brought a bigger net."

While the Gargantula went after the hunters, Fen helped Auggie get free. "You came for me!" Auggie said. "I *knew* you were my friend!"

"Um, no. I just didn't want the Professor to get angry at me for losing his stable boy."

Fen could say whatever he wanted. Auggie knew the truth.

Auggie picked up Willa, who was shivering.

"So that's a wisp, eh?" Fen said. "She's awfully . . . *wispy.*"

"She's fading away," Auggie said. "We have to get her out of here before the sun rises."

"Help!!!" A hunter shrieked as the Gargantula raised him above its giant mouth.

Auggie stood up. "*Gargantula,*" he said in his sternest voice. "We don't eat people."

GRRRWOOLLNN?

"Not even the bad ones," Auggie said. "How about you put him down, and then I'll give you as many oatmeal cookies as you want when we get home?"

The Gargantula licked her fangs. She tossed the hunter into the swamp and *galloomphed* back to the stables.

11

MISS BUNDT WAS WAITING AT THE GATE. "Sounds like I missed a bit o' fun."

Auggie set Willa down on the ground. The swamp had vanished. It was now a normal stall. "Welcome to the Fabled Stables," he said. "This is your new home."

Willa tried to lift her head. "Is this all mine?" Her voice was faint and trembly. "I love it."

Miss Bundt helped lead the Gargantula to her web.

"Glad to see you all made it back in one piece." She glanced at Willa, whose entire body was pale as mist. "And none too soon, I see."

Auggie looked through the side doors of the stables. The moon was sinking fast into the horizon. In a few moments, it would be gone. "The hunters who were after her said that when the moon disappears, she will disappear with it. Is that true?

"Afraid so," Miss Bundt said. "Wisps are moon critters. They are only meant to live for a single night."

"B-b-but I just got here," Willa said.

"There must be *something* we can do!" If only there were some way to stop the moon from disappearing.

Auggie looked out across the island. He got an idea . . . a teetering, towering idea!

MISS BUNDT'S LADDER HUNG FROM THE HORN OF THE
MOON. It swayed back and forth in the sky. "The next
time you ask me to help," Fen shouted, "Remind me
to say NO!"

"Hold still, I'm almost done!" Auggie chipped off a
tiny piece of moon. He tucked it in his pocket.

"Hurry!" Miss Bundt called from below. "She's
almost gone."

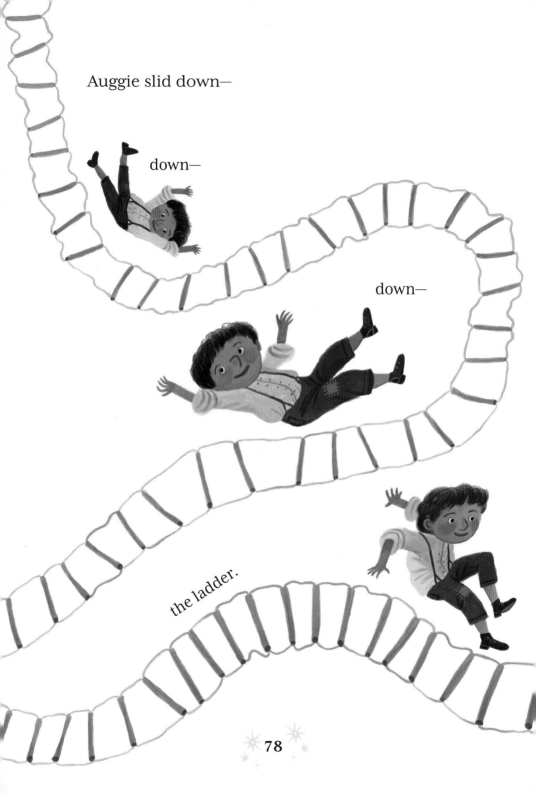

Auggie slid down—

down—

down—

the ladder.

Miss Bundt was waiting with Willa on the grass. The wisp was so pale that Auggie could hardly see her.

"Here," Auggie said, offering her the bit of moon. "Eat this." Willa was too weak to object.

Auggie and the others watched as she chewed and swallowed.

YIPPEEEEEEEEEEEEE

Auggie's face broke into a grin. "It worked!"

Willa twiddle-twirled in the air and dashed away.
"Catch-as-catch-can!"

"How do you like that?" Fen muttered. "Not even
a thank-you."

"Well done, the both of you!" Miss Bundt said. "That
bit o' moonshine should keep her fit and fighting for
years to come. The Professor would be proud."

EEEEEE!

Auggie watched Willa dance across the meadow. "Miss Bundt, do you think that Professor Cake knew we would need that ladder?"

Miss Bundt shrugged. "If he knew, he didn't tell me. A ladder's a useful thing in any situation. It happened to be extra useful tonight."

Willa was safe, but was she really free? That iron collar was still around her neck.

Auggie turned to Miss Bundt. "The people who were chasing her knew all about wisps and magical beasts. They had marks on their cloaks." He drew a picture in the dirt. "It looks like a little tower."

Miss Bundt's face tensed. "It's a rook." She released a heavy sigh. Miss Bundt's sighs made you want to sigh, too. "Professor Cake isn't the only one keen on finding one-of-a-kind things. But some of those other folks aren't interested in helping the critters they find. They only want to use 'em for their own dark ends." She brushed the dirt clean. "The Rooks are an old enemy, from well before my time. If the Rooks are back, then the stables are more important than ever."

Auggie imagined creatures across the Wide World, all running in fear. "The Rooks are trapping magical creatures?"

Miss Bundt rested a hand on his shoulder. "Not if we have anything to say about it."

Willa the Wisp bounded in front of Auggie, her bell ringing brightly. "Let's play hide-and-go-seek! I'll hide first!"

She zipped across the meadow in a trail of
blue smoke.

"Is she always like this?" Fen said.

Auggie smiled. "I hope so."

13

AT THE TOP OF THE WORLD SAT AN ISLAND.

At the heart of that island lived a boy named

Auggie . . .

And a Stick-in-the-Mud named Fen . . .

And a wisp named Willa . . .

And they were all friends!

WHAT ONE-OF-A-KIND CREATURE
WILL AUGGIE MEET NEXT?
FIND OUT IN THIS SNEAK PEEK
OF BOOK 2!

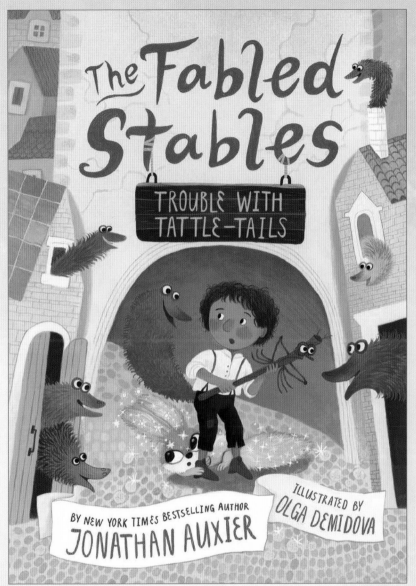

The Fabled Stables

TROUBLE WITH TATTLE-TAILS

BY NEW YORK TIMES BESTSELLING AUTHOR
JONATHAN AUXIER

ILLUSTRATED BY
OLGA DEMIDOVA

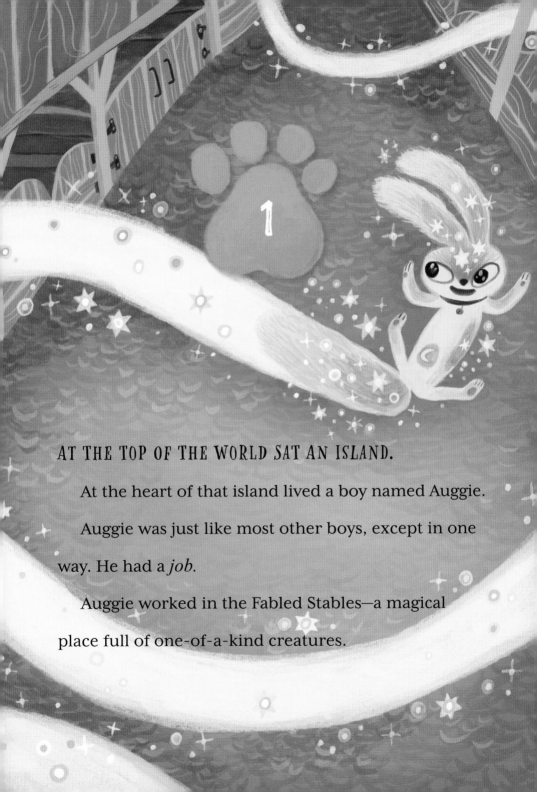

AT THE TOP OF THE WORLD SAT AN ISLAND.

At the heart of that island lived a boy named Auggie.

Auggie was just like most other boys, except in one way. He had a *job*.

Auggie worked in the Fabled Stables—a magical place full of one-of-a-kind creatures.

Usually Auggie loved his job. But not today. Today he had a problem.

Auggie was taking care of the Unfeeling Brute.

This was a tricky task, because Auggie had no idea what the Unfeeling Brute wanted from life. The creature had no eyes, no ears, no mouth, and no nose. Auggie was *pretty sure* it had a head, but he couldn't be certain.

Willa the Wisp drifted over. "Any luck?"

Auggie sighed. "Only bad luck."

Auggie flopped to the ground. "I've tried singing to her, feeding her, and taking her for a walk . . . but she won't respond."

"Maybe she wants to tickle fight?" Willa was always up for a good tickle fight.

Auggie picked up Fen and waved him in front of the Brute. "Maybe she wants to play fetch?"

Fen wriggled out of his grip. "*Maybe* the thing just wants to be left alone. *Some of us* like being left alone."

This was a rude thing to say, but what do you expect from a *literal* Stick-in-the-Mud?

2

AT THAT VERY MOMENT, IN A VILLAGE FAR AWAY,

a bell was *ding-ding-ding*ing as loud as loud could be.

It was an alarm bell.

It belonged to a bank.

A bank with an open front door.

Two thieves strolled through the halls. They wore dark cloaks with heavy hoods. They had loot sacks and lockpicks. They had plans and schemes.

There was a vault in the basement of the bank. A vault with a one-of-a-kind treasure. The thieves

walked into the vault and swiftly swept the treasure into their bags.

And why didn't the guards stop them?

That is a very good question.

AUGGIE WAS ON THE ROOF, cleaning out the Bizzybee hives.

He was still thinking about the Unfeeling Brute. "How do you help someone who doesn't want anything?"

Willa was trying to catch a Bizzybee in her paws. "Maybe Fen is right," she said. "Maybe we should just leave her alone?"

"OF COURSE I'M RIGHT!" Fen called from inside a hive.

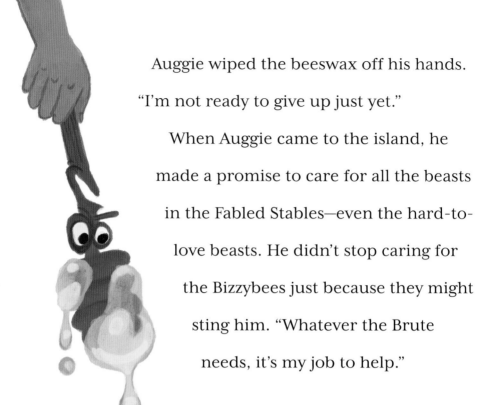

Auggie wiped the beeswax off his hands. "I'm not ready to give up just yet."

When Auggie came to the island, he made a promise to care for all the beasts in the Fabled Stables—even the hard-to-love beasts. He didn't stop caring for the Bizzybees just because they might sting him. "Whatever the Brute needs, it's my job to help."

"I know!" Willa said. "We can ask Professor Cake what to do!"

Professor Cake was the man who owned the island. He was very old and very clever. He was also very busy.

"I know I shouldn't bother the Professor," said Auggie, "but maybe just this once—"

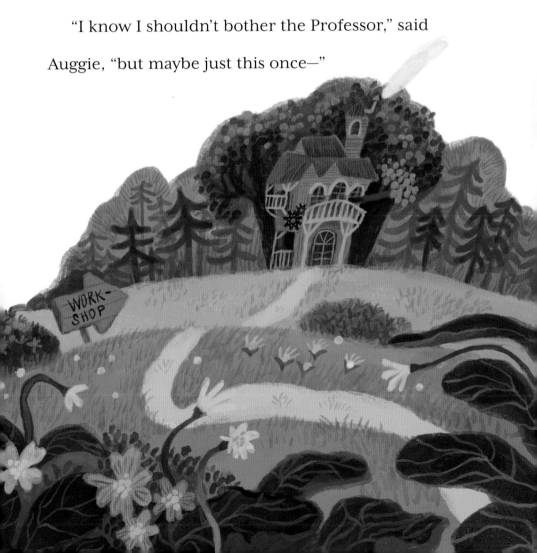

BOOM!

Suddenly, the stables SHOOK and SHUDDERED and TWITCHED and SPUTTERED.

A moment later, everything was still again.

Auggie picked himself up. He and Willa looked at each other.

"A new arrival!" they cried.

ABOUT THE AUTHOR

JONATHAN AUXIER is the *New York Times* bestselling and critically acclaimed author of *Peter Nimble and His Fantastic Eyes*, *The Night Gardener*, *Sophie Quire and the Last Storyguard*, and *Sweep*. He lives with his family in Pittsburgh, Pennsylvania. You can find him online at thescop.com.

ABOUT THE ILLUSTRATOR

OLGA DEMIDOVA studied at the Moscow Art Institute of Applied Arts. Olga started work as an animator, but her tremendous passion for illustration changed the direction of her work. Now she works with publishers from all over the world to illustrate books and apps, mostly for children.